THE
Sleeping
Rose

Published in Nashville, Tennessee, by Tommy Nelson™, a division of Thomas Nelson, Inc.
Executive Editor: Laura Minchew; Managing Editor: Beverly Phillips.

Library of Congress Cataloging-in-Publication Data

Hunt, Angela Elwell, 1957–
    The sleeping rose / by Angela Elwell Hunt ; illustrated by Chuck Gillies.
        p.   cm.
    Summary: While nurturing his beautiful rose, which the king invited him to show to the
entire kingdom, Baldrik learns the lesson that kindness is more important than praise.
    ISBN 0-8499-5847-4
    [1. Kindness—Fiction. 2. Roses—Fiction. 3. Christian life—Fiction.] I. Gillies, Chuck,
1950– ill. II. Title.
PZ7.H9115S   1998
[E]—dc21

98-13787
CIP
AC

Published in the United States of America

98 99 00 01 02 03 RRD 9 8 7 6 5 4 3 2 1

THE
Sleeping
Rose

Angela Elwell Hunt

Illustrated by Chuck Gillies

Thomas Nelson, Inc.

Nashville

Once within a faraway valley, Baldrik Macklin,
his wife, and two children lived on the outskirts of
a bustling and prosperous kingdom.

Baldrik raised beans, wheat, and barley during the warm months while his wife sewed lovely clothes for the village people. But in the springtime, Baldrik devoted his time to the care of a single rosebush, a strong plant that every year

produced only one flower. Baldrik's son, Jakob, called it the
May Day Rose, for though the blossom appeared in the early
spring, the flower always opened to its purest color and
sweetest fragrance on the first day of May.

Baldrik's daughter, Gretchen, said she had never seen a more
perfect rose. "'Tis as white as sunshine on snow, and as soft
as swan's down. Only a master gardener could grow such a
rose," she said. And all the villagers agreed.

"I'm not a master gardener," Baldrik modestly replied. "I'm just a farmer." But at night he dreamed of wearing silks and satins and tending the king's royal gardens.

Word of Baldrik's May Day Rose spread throughout the kingdom. One April day a sealed parchment arrived at the Macklin farm.

"Their Royal Highnesses, the King and Queen," the letter began, "request your presence at their May Day celebration. Bring your famous rose, so the entire kingdom can rejoice in its beauty."

Mrs. Macklin's mouth dropped open. "I must make us new clothes for the celebration. We must look our best, for surely you will become a royal gardener after this!"

Baldrik's heart began to beat faster. "I must see to the rose," he said.

He turned toward the gate where the plant was growing in a sunny spot, but gasped when he saw a beggar standing there.

The man's feet were tied up in rags, and his dirty hands were gently stroking the rosebush.

"Stop!" Baldrik cried, running. "Get away! Have you no consideration? Have you no feelings?"

"I only wanted—" the stranger began.

"I don't care! That rosebush is precious, with a right royal rosebud! Now get away, scat, shoo!"

The beggar hung his head and turned, but before he left Baldrik saw a single tear slide from the man's cheek and stain the rosebud. "Go!" Baldrik cried.

The next morning, Baldrik yawned and smiled, imagining all the wonderful things the king would say about his talent with flowers. Then he went outside to look at his May Day Rose. In a moment, Baldrik was back in the house.

"I'm a little worried," he told his family. "'Tis only two days until May first, and the rosebud hasn't begun to open."

"Don't worry, Papa," Gretchen said. "Perhaps the rosebush is a wee bit thirsty. Why don't you give it a drink?"

So Baldrik did.

That night he dreamed that the king dubbed him "Sir Baldrik, Knight of the Royal Gardens." He got up with the sun and went outside to look at his May Day Rose. In an instant, he was back in the house.

"I'm worried," he told his family. "The king's celebration is tomorrow night, and the rosebud still hasn't begun to open."

"Don't worry, dear," his wife said as she sewed a sleeve on his handsome new shirt. "Perhaps the rosebush is a wee bit chilly. Why don't you warm it with your cloak?"

So Baldrik did.

The next morning, while it was still dark, Baldrik climbed out of bed and went outside to look at his May Day Rose. In a flash, he was back in the house.

"Heaven help us!" he shouted. "Today is the king's festival, and the rosebush hasn't opened at all!"

Jakob opened his sleepy eyes and yawned. "Perhaps the rosebush is a wee bit lonely, Papa. Why don't you bring it inside?"

"How can a plant be lonely?" Baldrik frowned. "A bush has no more feelings than a rock, a tree, a beggar passing by—" He caught his breath. The beggar . . . had *cried*. Plants did not cry, nor did rocks or trees, but the beggar was a man in need, and Baldrik had sent him away. Baldrik's heart squeezed in sorrow. Surely a lonely man was more important than a single rosebud.

"I'll be home later," he told his wife. "Keep a pot of stew on the fire."

Baldrik left his cozy house and searched throughout the
countryside. He hiked across land as flat as stretched cloth,
then climbed over wrinkled hills where the ground gathered
itself into deep folds thickly laced with vines.

Finally, in a meadow near the road, he found the beggar
sleeping in the grass. "Come, friend." Baldrik slipped his cloak
around the man's thin shoulders. "My wife has dinner waiting
for us."

"My goodness, how hungry you both must be," Mrs. Macklin said when they arrived. She motioned toward the table. "Come in, both of you. Warm yourselves by the fire as you eat."

After dinner, Mrs. Macklin gave both men new shirts and breeches and soft cloaks. As the Macklins left the house to

journey to the king's palace, Baldrik glanced at the rosebush. The rosebud still had not opened.

"It doesn't matter," Mrs. Macklin whispered. "You have done good things today."

The royal celebration was everything the Macklins had dreamed it would be. Music and laughter filled the air as the king and queen led the dance of the Maypole.

After a grand feast, the king stood. The crowd fell silent, and Baldrik felt his heart sink as the king looked his way.

"Baldrik Macklin," the king's voice boomed over the crowd, "we have heard many wonderful reports about your May Day Rose. Now we would like to see this wondrous flower for ourselves."

Baldrik stepped forward on trembling legs. "I am sorry, Your
Majesty," he said, bowing, "but the rose has not yet bloomed."
Baldrik lowered his head in a silence that was the holding of a
thousand breaths.

"I thought you were a master gardener," the king's voice
rumbled. "I am sorely disappointed."

"Do not be disappointed in Baldrik Macklin, Your Highness." A different voice rang over the gathering, and Baldrik lifted his head.

"Baldrik sees what others cannot," the beggar said, coming forward with the emerald green bud in his hands. "When others turned me away, Baldrik searched and found me. He fed me from his table, and exchanged my rags for warm clothes. Only he cared enough to see my broken heart."

As the stranger spoke, tears of joy fell from his eyes onto the sleeping rosebud. Before the astonished gaze of the villagers, the rosebud frilled in the lamplight, spreading its snowy petals in a dazzling burst of brightness. The sweet fragrance of a thousand roses filled the air; the brilliant blossom burned in white-gold radiance.

As the king and queen gasped in amazement, the stranger turned and placed his hands on Baldrik's shoulders.

"You have chosen the right thing," the stranger said, a smile lighting his eyes. "People matter more than praise. Know this, Baldrik Macklin—anytime you offer help to a needy soul, you have offered it to me."

With great and gentle dignity the man turned and
walked away. As the crowd buzzed with the sound
of people exclaiming over the beauty of the radiant
rose, Baldrik marveled over the stranger's parting
words . . . and the tender touch of the man's
nail-scarred hands.